Almost
{Katharine the Great}

Bent Out
of Shape

Sarah ~
Stay in shape - read!
♡ Lisa Mullarkey

by Lisa Mullarkey
illustrated by Phyllis Harris

magic
wagon

visit us at www.abdopublishing.com

To a class act: Maureen + Curtin = Master Teacher² —LM

To Linda Stokes, thank you for your wonderful support and friendship through the years. —PH

Text by Lisa Mullarkey
Illustrations by Phyllis Harris
Edited by Stephanie Hedlund and Rochelle Baltzer
Interior layout and design by Jaime Martens
Cover design by Jaime Martens

Library of Congress Cataloging-in-Publication Data

Mullarkey, Lisa.
  Bent out of shape / by Lisa Mullarkey ; illustrated by Phyllis Harris.
    p. cm. -- (Katharine the almost great ; bk 4)
  ISBN 978-1-60270-582-1
  [1. Geometry--Fiction. 2. Schools--Fiction.] I. Harris, Phyllis, 1962- ill.
II. Title.
  PZ7.M91148Ben 2009
  [E]--dc22

                                                              2008036088

❋ CONTENTS ❋

❀ CHAPTER 1 ❀

Geometry Blues

I'm a super-duper straight-A student.

Except for math. Math is gross-a-rama report card drama. I'm getting back my first math test in third grade and I'm doomed!

Why? Because I stink-a-roo in math. My parents call me Katharine the *Almost* Great. They say I'm a work-in-progress. I bet if I could get an A in math, they'd call me Katharine the Great.

After unpacking my backpack, I headed straight to our classroom mailboxes and shoved my hand inside. I pulled out my test and took a quicky quick peek. I didn't see a C. Or a D. Or an F!

But there wasn't an A or a B either. Instead, there were oodles of Xs with new answers scribbled over my old ones. I didn't have time to count the Xs because I heard an itty-bitty noise behind me.

I spun around and saw Miss Priss-A-Poo smirking. "You got all those wrong?" Then she flashed her test with a big fat A and smiley face at me. "I got all mine right!"

I glanced back at my test. No smiley face.

Miss Priss-A-Poo tossed her hair and skipped away humming something that sounded like, "Katharine got an F. Katharine got an F."

I trudged back to my seat.

Miss Priss-A-Poo's real name is Vanessa. We were BFFs in kindergarten until:

1. Her mom started writing messages on her napkins and tucking them inside her lunch box.

2. She asked me to read them to her.

"What does this one say?" she asked while chomping on a carrot stick. Before I read it to her, I spied two yummy looking oatmeal cookies in her lunch box. Since Vanessa refused to swap-a-roo, I came up with another idea.

This is what the napkin said: *Have fun in gym today.*

But I told her it said: *Give Katharine two cookies.*

So she did.

The next day, she asked me to read another note. "What does this say?"

It said: *I hope you finger paint today.*

But I told her it said: *Give Katharine three pieces of bubblegum from your backpack.*

Vanessa scratched her head. "How did my mom know I had bubblegum?"

I shrugged. "Moms know *everything*."

When her napkin said: *Don't forget to return your library book*, I told her it said: *Katharine is your boss today. Do whatever she says.*

For the rest of the day, I made her color with me, trade her apple for my celery sticks, and play jump rope at recess.

My plan was per-fect-o until one day when Vanessa wouldn't let me near her napkin.

"My mom said *I* have to read this one to *you*," she barked. She cleared her throat and read: *Dear Katharine, You played a naughty trick on Vanessa. I'm calling your mother.*

Mrs. Garfinkle didn't just call my mom. She called Mrs. Ammer, our principal, too.

As I thought about that first visit to the principal's office, Mrs. Bingsley made an announcement.

"Today we're starting a new chapter in math. Geometry."

Everyone cheered. Including me. Shapes are easy breezy.

"We'll warm up a bit before we start." She passed out geoboards. "Use your rubber bands to make shapes."

Geoboards were fun! I stretched the first rubber band over four pegs and made a trapezoid.

Then, I added an upside-down one on top to make a pentagon. Or was it a hexagon? An octagon? At least I knew it made some type of *gon*.

Next, I made a car and showed Mrs. Bingsley. Vanessa whispered that my car looked like it was out of gas. So a minute later, I shot a rubber band at her.

When she glared at me, I gave her my very most innocent look. "Oops. Sorry."

A few minutes later, Mrs. Bingsley passed out colored paper shapes. We were supposed to use them to make geometric designs on construction paper. Rebecca asked me to work with her. We made a garden of flowers and used so many shapes that I felt dizzy.

We made round flowers, star flowers, and rectangular trees with circle tops. Then Rebecca said we needed hexagon, octagon, septagon, and decagon flowers.

I didn't know which were which, but Rebecca made them look beautiful. Then she did something amazing. She gathered up little squares, folded them zippity zip, and made tulips! Out of squares! She called it origami. I tried to make origami flowers, but they looked like crumply weeds.

When everyone saw our picture, they oohed and ahhed over Rebecca's origami flowers. No one mentioned my trees. My shoulders drooped. I felt like one of my crumply weeds.

Mrs. Bingsley drew triangles on the board. "Who knows this shape?"

She called on my cousin, Crockett. "It's a right triangle."

"Wrong, Crockett," I said. "It's a plain triangle."

"Actually," said Mrs. Bingsley. "Crockett's correct."

Mrs. Bingsley drew more triangles. She used words like *obtuse*, *acute*, and *equal* somethings. There were so many triangles, I felt tricked!

At lunch, I traded my mom's perfectly cut triangle-shaped tuna and pickle sandwich for Matthew's Fluffer-Nutter peanut butter one. I didn't care if Mom saw me.

"I hate triangles," I announced. "Geometry's stupid."

"Geometry's cool," said Miss Priss-A-Poo.

"Geometry's fun," said Crockett.

"Geometry is easier than multiplication," said Johnny Mazzaratti.

My stomach did a flip-flop belly drop. If geometry was so easy breezy, then why was I so bent out of shape?

❀ CHAPTER 2 ❀

Triangle Troubles

At recess, the boys played four square. The girls huddled around Rebecca and begged her to make origami flowers.

Crockett walked up to me and asked, "Want to play four square?"

"That game is a disgust-o math game," I said in a shaky voice. I folded my arms and stuck my nose in the air. "No thank you!"

He laughed. "Just because it has the word *square* in it doesn't mean it's a math game."

Then I acted like one of my favorite actors, Penelope Parks. "I do not adore it at all, Crockett. I simply *can't* play it."

He bounced the ball. "What if we changed the name?"

I rattled my head. "I'm boycotting shapes."

Boycotting was one of our vocabulary words in social studies. I felt sparkly for using it.

Instead of playing four square, I jumped into piles of fall leaves and crunched-a, crunched-a, crunched-a them under my feet.

I started to crunch-a, crunch-a to songs from our play, *Kids Rock in Space.* Tamara and Miss Priss-A-Poo saw how much fun I was having and jumped into my pile. They started to crunch-a, crunch-a to *Kids Rock in Space,* too.

"Guess this song," said Tamara. She stomped her feet.

"Easy," I said. "It's 'Mission Control.'"

Next, we crunched-a together to "The Milky Way Rock."

Miss Priss-A-Poo smirked. "Guess my song."

Her crunches didn't sound like any song from our class play. It went like this: Crun-cha, crun-cha, cruuunch. Crun-cha, crun-cha, cruuunch.

Tamara had no idea what song it was but I sure did. It was the "Katharine got an F" song. How rude!

I clenched my fists. My leaf-dancing days were over.

After recess, it was my very most favorite time of the day: story time!

Our carpet area is comfy cozy and filled with a bajillion books in buckets, baskets, and bookshelves. Besides the purplicious beanbag chair, there's a wilty, wrinkly blue one that looks destuffed.

During story time, Mrs. Bingsley would choose two kids to sit on the bags. Sometimes she'd pick someone who gave an extra brainy answer or showed extra self-control. I thought about the rubber band I shot at Miss Priss-A-Poo and my unbrainy math morning. I sighed.

Then I remembered that she'd also pick kids who were having total ick days. Today, that would be me!

I sat with a sad look on my face, hoping Mrs. Bingsley would realize that I needed the beanbag chair.

"Hmm," said Mrs. Bingsley as she scanned the carpet. Eighteen kids sat tall. Then she spotted slumpy, droopy me. I let out a loud sigh for effect. It worked!

"Katharine, how about you take a beanbag. Rebecca, you may chose one as well."

I flew over and ploppity plopped into the purplicious chair. I felt better already.

The feeling only lasted until Mrs. Bingsley held up the book she was about to read. It was not the next chapter of *The Coconut Caper*.

"This is *The Greedy Triangle* by Marilyn Burns. It's funny and will help you with geometry," she said.

Since I'd decided triangles were tricky, my ears clammed up and wouldn't listen to the story. Instead, I counted the polka dots on Mrs. Bingsley's shirt until my eyes got dizzy. Then, I picked at my Band-Aid on my knee until I felt a poke-a-roo in my back.

It was a manatee book sticking out from the shelf. I tugged on it and plopped it down next to the bag so no one could see it. I flipped through a few pages, then I heard someone say my name.

"Katharine," said Mrs. Bingsley, "what are you doing?"

I slid the book under the bookcase. "Just listening to *The Hungry Triangle*."

Everyone laughed. Everyone except Mrs. Bingsley. "It's *The Greedy Triangle*."

I rocked back and forth and fiddled with my earring.

"Well then, I suppose you can tell us about equilateral triangles," Mrs. Bingsley said.

I shrugged and looked at Crockett. He drew a triangle in the air and mouthed equal *something*.

This is what I thought Mrs. Bingsley would say:

"If you don't know the answer, you are going to fail math right now!"

Instead, she said:

"There is a clue in the word *equal*. Can anyone help Katharine?"

Eighteen hands shot into the air.

She called on Tamara. "It's when all sides of a triangle are the same length. Get it? *Equal.*"

Everyone stared at me. I waved.

Mrs. Bingsley sighed and motioned for me to sit by her. So I slid off of the purplicious beanbag chair and scooted over.

When it was time for music, I skedaddled to the front of the line. Everyone knows that the front of the line people get the best instruments to play.

When we got to the music room, I gave Mrs. O'Neil a super-duper smile.

"Well hello, Katharine," said Mrs. O'Neil. "Would you like the bongos or the triangle today?"

A no-brainer. I grabbed the bongos and spent the rest of music class banging my troubles away.

❀ CHAPTER 3 ❀

The Bermuda WHAT?!

"**W**hy so glum, chum?" Dad asked at dinner.

I shrugged and twirled spaghetti around my fork.

"Don't you feel well?" Mom asked. She wiped Jack's nose. "You could be catching Jack's cold."

On cue, Jack sneezed and strained peas and applesauce flew across the table. A goof-a-roo grin appeared on his face.

Babies are lucky ducks. No math tests or report card worries. I thought up a baby report card for Jack.

He'd make the honor roll!

"Well?" Dad said, interrupting my daydream.

"You have to sign a math test."

"Did you ace it?" asked Dad pointing to the Wall of Fame. The Wall of Fame is a ginormous wall in our kitchen where my parents hang up my fab-u-lo-so work. Right now, a dozen art projects and six tests are tacked to the board.

"Nope. Not even close. There wasn't a grade."

"No grade?" asked Mom. "That's odd." She laughed. "Maybe they're all wrong."

After she saw my super-serious face, she shrieked. "Katharine, you didn't get all of them wrong, did you?"

I twirled faster. "Did you know that there are more than 600 different pasta shapes in the world?" I shoved a forkful of spaghetti into my mouth. "What's your favorite?" I have a calendar of 365 useless facts that comes in handy during times like this.

"Katharine," said Mom, "did you get them *all* wrong?"

"Not *all* of them." I reached into my backpack on the chair. I yanked the test out of my folder and slid it across the table.

Mom studied it and passed it to Dad. Dad studied it and passed it to me.

I wanted to flush it down the toilet.

"It's mostly multiplication," said Dad. "You need to memorize your facts."

"But that's just it," I complained. "I've tried. It doesn't work. Math is disgust-o." I pushed my plate away.

"Did you study?" asked Dad.

"A little."

"Maybe you need to study *a lot*," said Mom.

I pointed to the Wall of Fame and jumped up. "Look at my last spelling test. I got an A+ and got the bonus word right." I showed off my talents by spelling Mississippi quicky quick. "Did you know I can spell supercalifragilisticexpialidocious?"

"We're not worried about your spelling," said Dad.

I yanked my science test and social studies report off the wall. "Both of these are As too." I stood and bowed. "Did you know I'm the only kid in class who can spell Mississippi *and* locate it on a map?"

My parents didn't look impressed.

"And look at my book report," I continued.

Mom hushed me. "We'd really like you to work harder in math, Katharine. What's the problem?"

I scrunched my nose. "*Problems* are the problems. I don't need math."

"Math is everywhere," said Dad. "You make forts with Crockett. Architects use math."

"You cook," added Mom. "Chefs use math skills all the time."

"Big deal," I said. "I won't be a chef or an architect." I curled my ponytail around my finger. "Besides, I'm still thinking about being a star."

"Even stars need math," said Dad. "You'll need to keep track of your money."

"Crockett will take care of my moola." Whenever we played Monopoly, he'd insist on being the banker because I gave out too much change.

Mom sighed. "You need a more positive attitude."

I rolled my eyes.

"I said you need a more positive attitude—not more *sassitude*."

Dad sucked in his breath, "Maybe she needs a tutor, Carol."

"A *tutor*? I don't need a tutor! Tutors are for kids who don't understand things." I pointed to the Wall of Fame.

"I'm a very smart third grader."

Mom nodded. "We agree. But math can be challenging. Why struggle?"

"Let me take one more test," I whined. "I'll get an A."

Mom wiped her mouth and then tossed her napkin onto her plate.

I thought she would say this:

"You *better* get an A."

But she didn't. She said:

"We'd be happy with a C for now as long as you're trying."

Just then Crockett hopped up the stairs. He and Aunt Chrissy live in our basement. I ran over to Crockett. "He'll tutor me in math."

"I can't even get you to play four square!" Then Crockett scooped something off of the counter and waved it in the air. "Who's going to Bermuda?"

"That would be me," said Dad. "I have a business trip tomorrow."

Dad works in advertising and gets to go to important places—like zoos.

"Are you nervous to fly over . . . ," Crockett paused. "IT?"

Dad laughed. "You don't believe in IT, do you?"

"What's IT?" I asked. I was hap-hap-happy we weren't talking about math anymore.

Crockett rubbed his hands together. "Well, IT is an area in the Atlantic Ocean where planes and boats have disappeared. If you go over the area in a boat or ship . . . *zap* you disappear forever."

"That's horrible," I said. "Is it true?"

Crockett nodded. "Look it up. Everyone knows about the Bermuda Triangle." He hugged my dad. "It was nice knowing you, Uncle Ted."

Bermuda *Triangle*?

My eyes stung.

I knew triangles were tricky. But who knew they were deadly?

❀ CHAPTER 4 ❀

Gee, I'm a Tree!

I tried to skip school so I'd have time to convince Dad to stay away from that nasty triangle. It didn't work.

"Unless you spew green stuff like Jack, you're going to school," said Dad. He kissed my cheek. "The Bermuda Triangle is a myth."

I gritted my teeth and walked to school.

When I got there, Mrs. Bingsley was writing *Polygons* and *Angles* on the board.

How many *gon* words were there? I wished those *gons* would be gone!

I asked to go to the library to do research. "It's an emergency," I said. "A matter of life and death."

Mrs. Bingsley raised her eyebrows. "Can it wait?"

I shook my head. "Emergencies can't wait."

She put her hand on my shoulder. This is what I thought she'd say:

"Go during free reading."

But this is what she really said:

"You look like you have a lot on your mind."

My eyes watered.

She winked at me. "No worries, Katharine." She scanned the class. "Crockett, please go to the library and help Katharine research something."

I heart Mrs. Bingsley!

Crockett knew exactly where the Bermuda Triangle books were.

"This is a good one," said Crockett when we got to the library. He flipped through the pages. "Look at Chapter 10."

Chapter 10 was *Myth Busters*. I read every word and felt an itty-bitty bit better.

"I told you not *everyone* believes it," said Crockett.

"*You* believe it," I said. "You think my dad will be zapped to smithereens."

He dug his foot into the carpet. "My mom doesn't. Your parents don't either."

When we checked out the book, I saw my kindergarten teacher, Mrs. Curtin. She's the best kindergarten teacher in the world.

"Hi, kids," Mrs. Curtin said.

I looked down at her feet and giggled. She had her bunny slippers on.

She glanced at my book. "The Bermuda Triangle, huh? You don't believe that stuff, do you?"

When Crockett mentioned all the ships and planes that have disappeared, I burst into tears.

Mrs. Curtin hugged me. "What's wrong?"

But I cried so much that Crockett had to explain everything.

She handed me a tissue. "Crockett, head back to class and tell Mrs. Bingsley that Katharine's with me."

She sat down at a table and pulled a chair out for me. "Your dad is not in danger from the Bermuda Triangle. I've flown over it three times and I'm still here. It's a silly myth." Then she crossed her heart and held up her fingers to promise.

"Do you believe in the Loch Ness Monster, Big Foot, or the Abominable Snowman?" she asked.

I rolled my eyes. "Nope."

"Well, the Bermuda Triangle is just as silly."

I felt so much better that I leaned over and gave Mrs. Curtin a hug-a-rooni.

She asked, "Is there anything else wrong?"

"I hate triangles," I sighed. "Fat ones, thin ones, and Bermuda ones." I blew my nose. "Math is disgust-o."

"Maybe I can help. I know a few geometry tricks."

"Since triangles are tricky," I said. "I need tricks . . . and help."

She drew a triangle on a pad of paper. "This is a right triangle because its angle is at 90 degrees. Ninety-degree angles have perfect Ls in them." She dragged her pencil over the L. "Just remember that if you see an L, even if it's upside-down or on its side, it's a right angle."

Mrs. Curtin drew oodles of triangles. I found the L every time!

"Now those thin ones," she began. "The angle is smaller than an L." She stopped drawing. "Think of a baby for little angles. When people see you at the park with Jack, what do they say?"

"That he's cute."

"Exactly! *A cute* baby," said Mrs. Curtin. "It's an *acute* angle. Small equals cute. Get it?"

I did!

Then she rummaged through her purse and took out a picture.

"Spoinky!" I shouted. Spoinky is Mrs. Curtin's fat cat.

"That's right," Mrs. Curtin whispered, putting her finger to her puckered lips. "Shhh . . . Do you remember what word I used to describe him?"

An easy breezy question. "Obese," I said.

Mrs. Curtin always had a word of the week on a bulletin board. When the word was *obese*, she had Spoinky's picture under it.

"Do you remember what obese means?" she asked.

I blew my nose again. "Fat."

"Exactly!" squealed Mrs. Curtin. "If you see an angle bigger or fatter than a right triangle, it's ob . . ."

"Obese?" I asked.

She wrinkled her nose. "Not exactly. It's *obtuse*."

"Obtuse," I repeated.

She gathered up her paper.

"Here's a math joke to share with your class. What did the parrot say when he flew out of the cage? Poly-gone. Poly-gone."

"POLYGON!" I laughed.

She told another. "What did the acorn say when he grew up?"

I shrugged.

"Gee, I'm a tree," she said.

I thought about it. *Gee, I'm a tree . . . Gee, I'm a tree . . . GEOMETRY*! "Good one, Mrs. Curtin."

When I got back to class, everyone was identifying triangles.

"This is the last one," said Mrs. Bingsley. "What type of angle is this?" She looked right at me. "Katharine?"

"It's a Jack angle."

Kids laughed and whispered.

My face turned red. "I meant an *acute* angle."

"Excellent," said Mrs. Bingsley.

Then I taught everyone the tricks and jokes I learned from Mrs. Curtin.

Miss Priss-A-Poo and Johnny liked the jokes so much, they wrote them down.

I felt better until I saw the Bermuda Triangle book on the floor by Crockett's desk.

My stomach did a flip-flop belly drop. What if the joke was on me?

❁ CHAPTER 5 ❁

The Kitchen Triangle

A s soon as Crockett and I got home, I rush-a-rooed inside. "Is Dad in Bermuda yet?"

Mom and Aunt Chrissy were playing peekaboo with Jack. "He should be there soon," said Mom. "He promised to call the second he lands."

I slumped against the wall. "What if he doesn't call? What if the Bermuda—"

Mom didn't let me finish. "No worries, Katharine. He'll call."

Aunt Chrissy plopped a plate of cookies on the table.

I snatched one. "Did Mrs. Curtin talk to you, Mom?"

She nodded. "Why didn't you come to the cafeteria to get me?"

I shrugged and gave Jack a big kiss. "You're a cutie." Then I remembered Mrs. Curtin's geometry tricks and jokes and told Mom and Aunt Chrissy.

"Mrs. Curtin is one smart teacher," said Aunt Chrissy. She shot Mom a funny look.

Crockett laughed and held up a cookie. "She's one smart *cookie*."

The doorbell rang. A minute later, Mrs. Curtin and her bunny slippers were in my kitchen. I'd never had a teacher in my house before!

"Hi, Mrs. Curtin." I giggled. "Did you know a male rabbit is called a buck and a female is a called a doe?"

"Thanks for telling me." She winked at Mom and reached for one of her famous cookies. "I wanted to make sure you're okay, Katharine. Would you mind if I look over your math homework with you?"

I pulled my workbook out of my backpack and handed it to her.

She flipped through it. "Looks like you'll be learning about concave and convex shapes tomorrow."

I shoved my hands into my pockets. "That sounds hard."

"Not if you know the tricks." She turned the page. "You're going to learn about 3-D shapes, too."

"They're easy breezy," I said. I looked up and noticed that Crockett, Mom, and Aunt Chrissy had vanished. *Poof!* Maybe there was a *Kitchen Triangle.*

Mrs. Curtin grabbed a pad of paper. "You'll have to identify the bases, vertices, edges, and faces on 3-D objects."

My heart sank. "I've never even *heard* of vertices."

She reached into her bag and pulled out a wooden pentagon. She ran her finger along the edges and pointed out all of the vertices, faces, and the base.

It was fun learning about different polygons. I was sad when Mom magically reappeared. "Mrs. Curtin, don't you have to be getting home?"

Mrs. Curtin leaned over and whispered two more jokes in my ear. Then she said, "Time flies when you're visiting friends."

When she said *friends*, I felt sparkly. A second later, the phone rang.

"Hi, Uncle Ted," said Crockett.

I zip-a-zoomed to the phone and jumped for joy when I heard Dad's voice. I only got to talk to him for five minutes before Mom wrestled the phone away.

When I came back to the kitchen, Mrs. Curtin wasn't there. The Kitchen Triangle had struck again!

"Mrs. Curtin had to leave," said Aunt Chrissy. "Crockett went to get his skateboard. He said he'll meet you outside."

I skipped outside hap-hap-happy!

"How's your dad?" asked Crockett as he swerved around me.

"Per-fect-o! Alive and zap-free," I said. "He escaped the space aliens and sea monkeys."

Crockett hopped off of his board. "I think it's cool that Mrs. Curtin is tutoring you."

Tutoring me? Mrs. Curtin? Did aliens and sea monkeys zap Crockett's brain?

I laughed. "That's silly, Crockett. Mrs. Curtin wasn't tutoring me. She stopped by to—" then my stomach felt like rockets rumbling into space.

I swallowed hard. "I'm being tutored?" I felt tricked. "By a *kindergarten* teacher?"

Crockett shuffled his feet. "Well, if she's a teacher and she came to help you with math, she's tutoring you."

I stomped inside. Mom and Aunt Chrissy were making dinner. "Is Mrs. Curtin my *tutor*?" I demanded.

Aunt Chrissy sucked in her breath. "I think I'll head downstairs and give you ladies some privacy."

Mom wiped her hands on her apron. "Katharine, when Mrs. Curtin stopped by the cafeteria she told me how upset you were. She also mentioned that she had helped you with math. So, I asked her to stop by."

"She's a *kindergarten* teacher," I shouted. The kids will laugh. They'll call me goo-goo ga-ga girl."

"I'm not telling anyone," said Mom. "Aunt Chrissy won't either."

Crockett bounced into the kitchen. "I won't spill the beans either."

Mom hugged me. "Work with her for a few days. If you decide she's not helping, we'll stop."

I leaned against the Wall of Fame and spied my very first math paper of the year on it.

"What's that doing up there?" I asked. "There's lots wrong."

"But there's lots right. Mrs. Curtin said you worked really hard in the library to learn about angles. She said you earned an A for effort."

I thought about Mrs. Curtin. She was a fab-u-lo-so teacher.

"Want to hear a joke?" I asked.

I didn't wait for anyone to answer. "Who invented fractions?"

Crockett shrugged.

"Henry the Eighth," I said.

They chuckled.

"Who invented the round table?"

Mom guessed wrong.

I shouted, "Sir Cumference!"

Even though I didn't understand the joke, they sure did.

I started to like this joke telling.

When I went to bed that night, I fell asleep wondering if comedians had math-free jobs.

❁ CHAPTER 6 ❁

$\overline{MA}\ \overline{TH}$
$\overline{GE}\ \overline{TS}$
$\overline{ME}\ \overline{AN}$

When Mrs. Bingsley asked us to take out our workbooks for math, I pulled mine out quicky quick.

"We have lots to learn today," said Mrs. Bingsley. She drew polygons on the board. "Polygons come in all sorts of shapes. Some are concave. Some are convex."

I raised my hand. "Concave polygons are shapes that have at least one side that falls in. It's like someone pushed it in. Convex polygons have all sides pushed out."

Mrs. Bingsley looked surprised and handed the chalk to me. "Draw a circle around the concave polygons, please."

I rushed to the board and circled three shapes. "Can I tell the class a trick I know to remember the difference?"

"Sure, Katharine. Tips are helpful."

"Think about building a sandcastle on the beach. The sides usually cave in like this." I held my arms out and then bent them at my elbow. "That's how you'll remember con*cave* polygons."

Mrs. Bingsley smiled. Maybe I'd get the purplicious beanbag chair today for being so smart!

Then she introduced vertices, faces, edges, and bases. When she held up a solid 3-D shape, I identified all the parts!

For once I felt like a smarty in math. But not everyone did. Tamara, Rebecca, and Matthew had lots of questions.

"While I'm helping students," said Mrs. Bingsley, "I want everyone to draw and label line segments. I'm not asking for rays. Use the line segment symbol."

I looked at Miss Priss-A-Poo and smiled. She didn't smile back.

She growled. "How do you know so much now?"

"I'm a smarty," I said and laughed. She still didn't crack a smile.

"Are you jealous?" I asked. Vanessa is the best math student in our class. I figured she was upset that I got everything right.

But I had a secret. I only got everything right because Mrs. Curtin tutored me.

Vanessa scribbled on her paper and pushed it to the edge of her desk for me to see.

This is what I saw:

$$\overline{KC}$$
$$\overline{IS}$$
$$\overline{NO}$$
$$\overline{TA}$$
$$\overline{SM}$$
$$\overline{AR}$$
$$\overline{TY}$$

It was a secret code. It said Katharine Carmichael is not a smarty! How rude!

I quickly made my line segment codes and showed her:

$$\overline{VG}$$
$$\overline{IS}$$
$$\overline{DI}$$
$$\overline{SG}$$
$$\overline{US}$$
$$\overline{TO}.$$

Miss Priss-A-Poo looked confused. She may be the best math student in class but she's not a good reader. I whispered, "It says Vanessa Garfinkle is disgust-o."

She tossed her hair and turned her chair away from me.

When no one else needed help, Mrs. Bingsley announced, "Now we're going to see how much you remember about 3-D shapes." She held up toothpicks and a bag of mini-marshmallows.

"I'm going to pass out toothpicks and marshmallows. You'll construct as many 3-D shapes as you can." She picked up a toothpick and shoved a little marshmallow onto it. She speared another toothpick into that. Ten toothpicks later, she had a cube!

Everyone gave Mrs. Bingsley a round of applause.

"I'm going to give everyone their own pack of toothpicks and a half bag of marshmallows. I know it looks like a lot, but it's not. Depending on the size of your shapes, you might need dozens of marshmallows. So," she paused, "do not eat them. Got it?"

Nineteen kids shouted, "Got it!"

Marshmallows are one of my very most favorite foods. I only made three shapes before I started popping handfuls of puffy nuggets into my mouth.

When I looked around, I noticed that everyone else had way more shapes than I did. But I didn't have any more marshmallows!

Vanessa did.

"Can I have some of your marshmallows, Vanessa?" I asked in my most friendly voice.

She pointed to my line segment page. "No way."

Before I asked anyone else, a hand swooped down on my desk and whisked away my paper.

"Katharine," said Mrs. Bingsley, "does this say what I think it says?"

I bit my lip. "Did you know that Americans buy more than 90 million pounds of marshmallows a year and most are sold in October and December?"

She tapped her fingers on my desk. "I'm waiting for an answer."

"Vanessa started it," I said. "Look at her paper."

Mrs. Bingsley scanned Vanessa's paper. She handed it to me. "It doesn't say anything."

And it didn't. It said:

$$\overline{KO}$$
$$\overline{TS}$$
$$\overline{NO}$$
$$\overline{FA}$$
$$\overline{SN}$$
$$\overline{AR}$$
$$\overline{FY}$$

She changed her segments! No fair.

Mrs. Bingsley crumpled up my paper and tossed it into the trash.

No beanbag chair for me.

Instead, she pointed to the thinking chair because I was in:

$$\overline{BI}$$
$$\overline{GT}$$
$$\overline{RO}$$
$$\overline{UB}$$
$$\overline{LE.}$$

❀ CHAPTER 7 ❀

Cheatie Girl

At exactly four o'clock, Mrs. Curtin and her bunny slippers arrived with a bag of supplies.

"How was math today?" she asked.

"Per-fect-o," I said. I decided not to mention my line segment problems and trip to the thinking chair. "I taught the class the concave trick."

"Good for you, Katharine," said Mrs. Curtin. She flipped through her notes.

"I spoke to Mrs. Bingsley after school," Mrs. Curtin began.

I slouched in my chair. Did she know about my *Vanessa Garfinkle is disgust-o* line segments?

She continued, "You have a quiz tomorrow, don't you?"

I groaned. "I hate quizzes. I've been getting bad grades."

"But now you know lots of tricks," said Mrs. Curtin. "You'll do well if you study." She slid her feet out of her bunny slippers and wiggled her toes. "Shall we?"

We studied until I spotted Crockett and Johnny in the yard.

They caught me looking and waved. "Duck!" I yelled to Mrs. Curtin.

Mrs. Curtin quacked like a duck.

I pulled her down. "No, *duck* so they can't see you."

She blinked fast. "So *who* can't see me?"

I didn't want to hurt her feelings but I blurted out, "I can't be seen with you. You're a *kindergarten* teacher."

She didn't smile but she didn't get mad either. "Right now, I'm just a friend helping another friend work on math." Then she added, "*Third* grade math. Not kindergarten math."

Mrs. Curtin closed the blinds. "Katharine, you're not the only student I tutor. I work with lots of kids in all grades."

"Do you tutor anyone else in my class?"

She raised her shoulders. "If I did, I wouldn't tell you."

Who told her I'm a blabbermouth?

She straightened up. "I wouldn't tell anyone that I tutored you either because it's private. Top secret information."

"I like it that way," I said.

The next morning, I got up extra early to study.

"Haven't you studied enough?" Mom asked.

"Don't you want me to get a 100?"

I thought she'd say this:

"Of course. You better get a 100 with all your extra help."

But she said this:

"Nope. I just want you to do your best."

As soon as school started, Mrs. Bingsley passed out the quiz. I was done quicky quick. I looked around but since no one else was finished, I checked over my answers.

Miss Priss-A-Poo noticed me looking around. She covered her paper and mouthed *Cheatie Girl*.

I stuck my tongue out at her and handed in my paper.

After lunch, Mrs. Bingsley had a surprise for us. She passed out our math quiz from today and our reading test from yesterday.

"You may spend the next five minutes looking over your papers. If you have any questions, ask."

I flipped my reading paper over first. Another A.

My hand shook as I sneaked a peek at my math paper. I held it up to the light first and saw a smiley face! I also saw my grade. I got a 97!

I jumped up and down! "Crockett, I got a 97!"

He gave me two thumbs-up.

I pumped my fists in the air. "I'm a smarty!"

Miss Priss-A-Poo showed me her paper. She got a 97, too. "You cheated. You're a Cheatie Girl. You looked at my paper."

I put my hands on my hips. "I did not! I was done first." Then I saw her reading test. She had a 100 just like me.

Vanessa does not get 100s in reading. Ever.

I grabbed her reading test. *"You're* the Cheatie Girl. *You* copied off of *me.* That's the only way you could get a 100 on this test."

Mrs. Bingsley rushed over. "Girls! Stop this arguing right now. What's all the fuss about?"

"She cheated," said Vanessa. "She got the same math grade as me and I saw her looking around."

I huffed and puffed. *"You're* the Cheatie Girl. I studied hard. If you hate reading, how did you get a 100 on *The Coconut Caper* test?"

Mrs. Bingsley grabbed our hands and marched us out into the hall. She waited for Ms. Cerra, our second grade teacher, to pass by before she narrowed her eyes and gave us *the look.* She didn't say a word. Her eyes said it all.

I swayed back and forth. I needed to use the bathroom, but I used my common sense. I did not ask her for a bathroom pass.

Finally, I squeaked out, "Sorry."

"Sorry," whispered Vanessa.

Mrs. Bingsley squinted. "I'm disappointed in both of you. To hear both of you accusing each other of cheating is upsetting! Both of you earned your grades."

She looked down the hall. "I'm not quite sure what to do about this."

"How about I write *I'm sorry* 100 times?" I suggested.

Mrs. Bingsley shook her head.

Vanessa said, "I'll write it 1,000 times."

I gave Vanessa the evil eye. "I'll write it 2,000 times."

"Enough," said Mrs. Bingsley as she pointed down the hall.

"Mrs. Ammer's office?" asked Vanessa.

"Yes," said Mrs. Bingsley.

Great. Even my very first A in math wasn't enough to keep me from another visit with Ammer the Hammer.

If I had Mrs. Curtin's slippers, I'd hop, hop, hop away.

❀ CHAPTER 8 ❀

The Secret's Out

Mrs. Tracy smiled when we walked into the office. "What can I do for you girls?"

"We're here to see Mrs. Ammer," said Vanessa. "We're in trouble."

Mrs. Tracy's smile faded. "Have a seat over there."

A minute later, the phone rang.

Mrs. Tracy answered it and glanced at us. "Okay, I'll do that," she said. She swiveled her chair around and whispered something else into the phone. She was talking about us!

I crossed my fingers and hoped Mom wasn't about to drop off snacks or sign out for the day. She would not be happy if she knew I was visiting Mrs. Ammer again.

We waited for 15 minutes before Mrs. Tracy stood. "Girls, Mrs. Ammer isn't in today."

I jumped up and headed toward the door. "See ya!"

"Not so fast," said Mrs. Tracy. "Come with me."

Vanessa looked scared. She pushed me ahead of her.

Mrs. Tracy took us inside Mrs. Ammer's office and sat us down at her conference table. "Someone will be in to see you in a minute. Sit tight until then."

When Mrs. Tracy left, Vanessa started to cry. "I've never been sent to the principal before."

"Don't cry. I get sent a lot and it's not so bad. Besides, she's not even here."

Vanessa couldn't stop crying. "Who's coming to see us?"

"It better not be my mom," I said as I handed Vanessa a tissue. "Maybe it's Mrs. Bingsley."

Miss Priss-A-Poo blew her nose. "How did you get a 97 on the test?"

"I studied fair and square," I said. "I'm not a Cheatie Girl." Then I leaned back in the chair and put my feet on the table.

Vanessa rolled her eyes.

"Well, how did you get a 100 on the reading test? You don't like reading."

"I studied fair and square, too," said Vanessa.

Now I rolled my eyes at her.

The door creaked open. It was Mrs. Curtin!

We both jumped out of our chairs and gave her hug-a-roonies.

"Mrs. Ammer isn't here today," I said.

"I know," she said. "I came to see both of you."

"Both of us?" asked Vanessa. "Why?"

I was confused too. It was like the first day of geometry all over again! "How did you know we were here?"

She sat down. "Girls, I heard some upsetting news. Mrs. Bingsley said that you two were fighting over your test scores. That seems out of character for both of you. I'm disappointed."

Vanessa and I sat there silently.

"You should be celebrating each other's scores, not accusing each other of cheating." She turned toward me. "Did you study your hardest and deserve that 97?"

She knew I did. I studied with her! "Cross my heart!"

Then she turned toward Vanessa. "Did you study hard and earn that 100 all by yourself?"

Vanessa nodded and started crying again. "You know I studied, Mrs. Curtin. You helped me!"

"What?" I shouted. "Mrs. Curtin helped you?"

"Now you know my secret, Katharine. Mrs. Curtin tutors me in reading. That's why I've been doing so much better lately. It's not because I looked at your paper. Honest."

Then she put her head on the table. "I bet you don't believe me."

"I do, I do!" I shouted. "I do believe you." I laughed.

Vanessa made a grouchy face at me. "Are you laughing because I'm being tutored by a *kindergarten teacher*?"

"Nope. I'm laughing because Mrs. Curtin tutors me, too! She helped me with those tricky triangles and angles. She's the reason why I know all those geometry tricks and jokes."

Vanessa wiped her eyes and started to laugh. "I won't tell your secret if you don't tell mine."

I nodded. "Pinky promise?" Then I added, "I have a funny feeling she tutors lots of kids we know."

I turned around. "Right, Mrs. Curtin?" But Mrs. Curtin had vanished!

"Where did she go?" Vanessa asked. "It's like the Bermuda Triangle you talked about."

Even though I knew there was no such thing as the Bermuda Triangle, I made creepy eyes and wiggled my fingers in front of my face.

"Maybe the aliens and sea monkeys zapped her," I said.

Vanessa and I laughed as we walked back to our classroom. We weren't BFFs again, but now we were friends who shared a super-duper secret.

Be a Math Comedian

Mrs. Curtin's jokes helped Katharine learn math and were a super-duper hit with her class! If your friends are having a disgust-o math day, tell them these jokes to make them smile:

1. Where did the math student eat his lunch?
   At the multiplication table!

2. Why was the obtuse angle upset?
   Because he was never right!

3. What is a polar bear's favorite shape?
   An ICE-osceles triangle!

4. How do you catch a Geometrysaurus rex?
   With a Zoid Trap. The same way you would trap-a-zoid!

5. What do you call a crushed angle? *A rectangle!*

6. Why was the math book so sad? *It had a lot of problems!*